GIVE ME BACH MY SCHUBERT

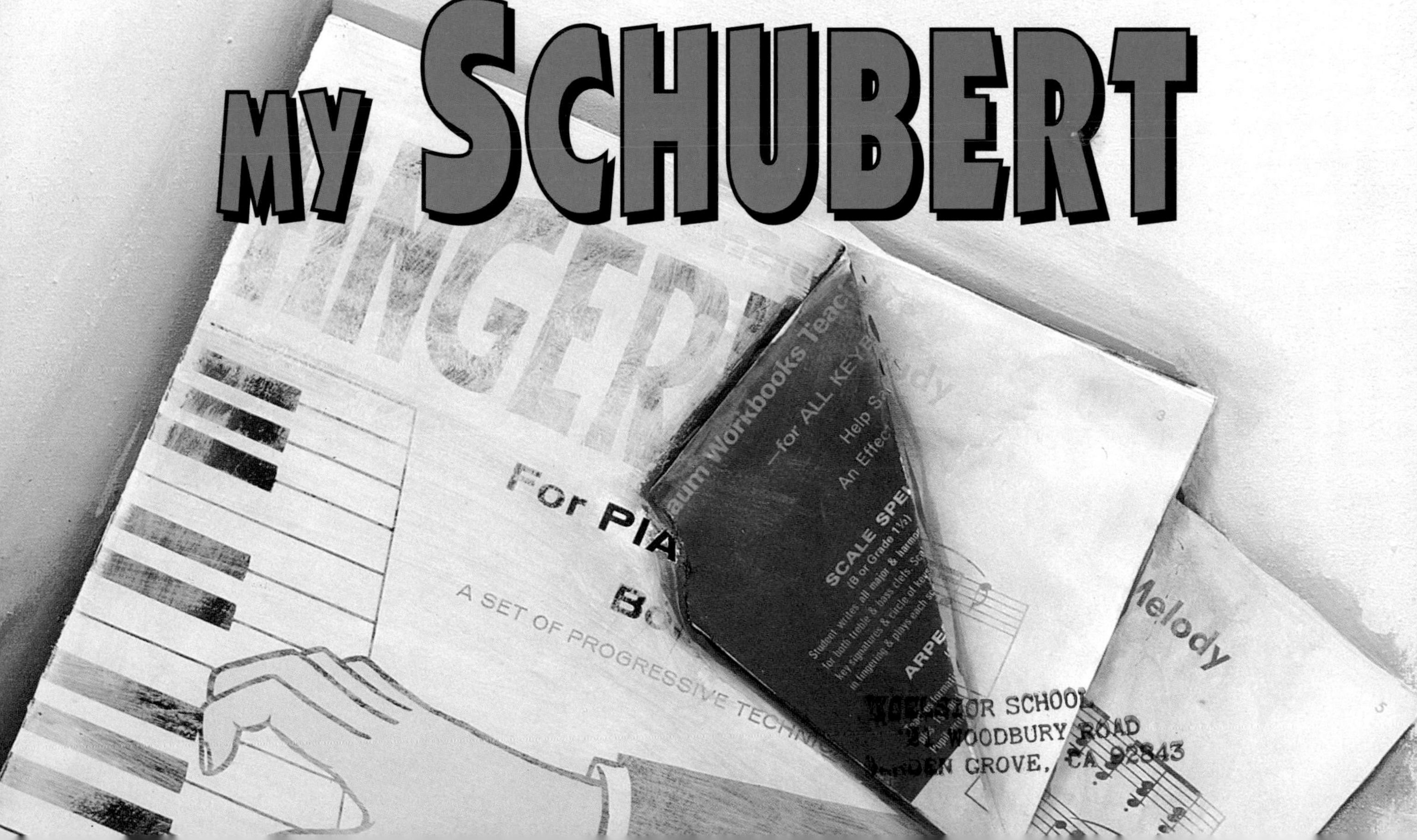

GIVE ME BACH MY SCHUBERT

by BRIAN P. CLEARY

illustrated by
RICK DUPRÉ

LERNER PUBLICATIONS COMPANY / MINNEAPOLIS

Library of Congress Cataloging-in-Publication Data

Cleary, Brian P., 1959–
  Give me Bach my Schubert / by Brian P. Cleary ; illustrated by Rick Dupré.
    p. cm.
  Summary : In a humorous rhyming verse filled with musical puns a boy tries
to run from a piano lesson.
  ISBN 0–8225–2116–4
  [1. Music—Fiction. 2. Puns and punning—Fiction. 3. Stories in rhyme.]
  I. Dupré, Rick, ill. II. Title.
  PZ8.3.C555Gi 1996
  [Fic]—dc20   94–32431

Manufactured in the United States of America
1 2 3 4 5 6 – JR – 01 00 99 98 97 96

For Grace, Ellen, and Emma—
the Fun Girls

B.P.C.

For my sister Debbie, who still helps me
do cartwheels

R.D.

My buddy Bert likes Haydn things—
he's sometimes hard to Handel.
I said, "Give me BACH my Schubert,"
'cause I knew he hid my sandal.

My friend Ray borrows books to reed
and balls to PITCH and throw.
I keep good *notes*, and sol fa re
owes mi a la ti do.

My uncle **Waltz** a shepherd,
and his flock is down to half.
He needs some help to keep his sheep,
and so he'll get a **staff**.

My grandma chops a *chord* of wood
and stacks it all by hand.
"I'd try to do some more, but, boy,
that's psalm my ax can stand!"

When crossing streets she warns us,
"There could be **A major** loss,
'cause if you don't **C-sharp**, you could
B-flat before you cross."

My friends the twins look so alike
that some chimes I forget—
I often think Annette is Claire,
or I'll call CLARINET.

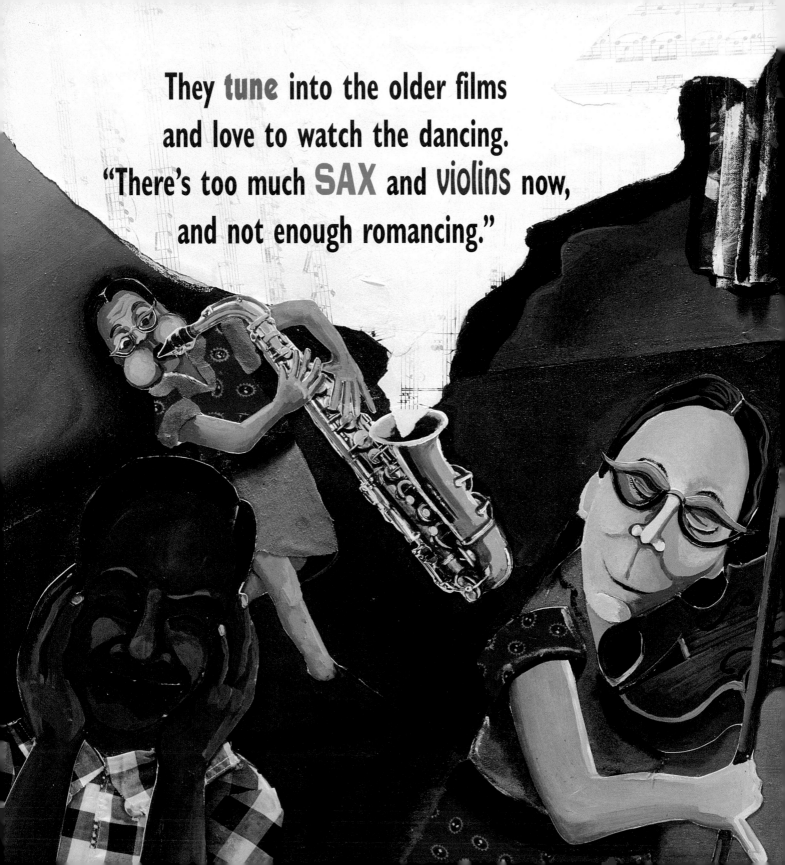

They **tune** into the older films
and love to watch the dancing.
"There's too much **SAX** and violins now,
and not enough romancing."

I always pick the scary films—
the dark, grotesque, and gory.
They often make me **FRET** at night,
but that's *sonata* story.